Barbie™ SOCCER COACH

By Barbara Slate
Illustrated by Art Ruiz,
Nancy Stevenson, and
Josie Yee

 A GOLDEN BOOK · NEW YORK

Golden Books Publishing Company, Inc., Racine, Wisconsin 53404

"You've got the look, Barbie!" exclaimed Skovoola.

Barbie turned, posed, and smiled for Skovoola's camera. *Click! Click!*

"That was lovely, Barbie!" agreed Jessica, editor of *Here Comes the Bride* magazine.

Skovoola handed his camera to an assistant. "It's always a pleasure to work with you, Barbie," he said.

"Well," said Barbie, "I have to run. I don't want to be late for my Tigers."

"Tigers?" asked Skovoola. "At the zoo?"

Barbie laughed. "No. I'm the coach of a girls' soccer team called the Tigers. Tomorrow is our big game against the Bears. If we win, I'm surprising my team with a victory party on the beach!"

Barbie waved good-bye to Skovoola and Jessica from her convertible.

"Good luck, Coach Barbie!" shouted Skovoola.

"It's going to take a lot more than luck to beat the Bears!" Barbie thought to herself as she drove away.

When Barbie arrived on the soccer field, the Tigers
were warming up.

"Before we start practice, I want to tell you to play your
best tomorrow," she said. "And always be a good sport."

"What if we lose the game?" asked Alexis.
"It doesn't matter," Barbie replied. "What's important
is how you play the game. And don't forget to have fun!"

Skipper and Alexis practiced passing the ball. "I really want to beat those Bears tomorrow," Alexis told Skipper.

"Don't worry, we will!" answered Skipper. She kicked the ball to Courtney.

"Good kick!" Barbie called to her little sister.

Finally it was the morning of the big game!
"Go, Tigers, GO!" shouted the Tiger fans.
The referee blew the whistle and the game began.

Courtney got the ball and passed it to Skipper. She passed it to Alexis, who kicked it into the Bear net for a goal.

The Tigers had the lead! "WAY TO GO, TIGERS!" shouted the fans.

Soon a Bear player named Stephanie had control of the ball. She took it down the field and kicked it right past the Tiger goalie!

"Great shot!" shouted the Bear coach.

The score was now tied at 1-1.

The game continued. Skipper ran up the field dribbling the ball. As Coach Barbie watched, Stephanie jammed her elbow into Courtney's side.

"Ow!" cried Courtney. "That hurt!"

Later in the game Alexis was passing the ball to a teammate when Stephanie pushed her from behind. Alexis fell flat.

"What are you doing?" asked Alexis angrily.

"Oh, sorry," said Stephanie with a laugh. "Maybe next time you'll learn to stay out of my way."

At halftime Barbie was surrounded by her team.
"Coach, the Bears are playing a dirty game!" cried
Alexis. "If we want to win, we should play that way, too!"
"We're going to play a good clean game," replied
Barbie. "If we play dirty and win, then we're still losers."

Barbie turned to the referee. "It's really getting rough out there," she said.

The referee blew his whistle. "This is a warning," he told the Bears. "Play clean or I'll call a foul!"

No one heard the Bear coach say to his team, "Do whatever it takes to win this game. WIN! WIN! WIN!"

At the beginning of the second half, Skipper got control of the ball and took it down the field. A Bear player named Donna stuck out her foot and tripped her! Barbie ran onto the field.

"Are you okay, Skipper?" she asked.

"My ankle hurts," answered Skipper.

"Foul against the Bears!" shouted the referee. "Free kick for the Tigers!"

Courtney kicked the ball as hard as she could, but the Bear goalie blocked the shot and sent the ball sailing back onto the field. The score remained tied at 1-1.

Alexis was angry when she heard that Skipper was out for the rest of the game with a twisted ankle.

"I don't care what Barbie says," she thought. "The Bears hurt my friend on purpose. I'm going to play just like them!"

With only a minute left in the game, the score was
still tied 1-1. Alexis ran down the field next to Donna.
Quickly, Alexis elbowed Donna, but the referee saw her.
"Foul!" he shouted. "The Bears get a free kick!"

Barbie called a time-out and motioned for Alexis to come over.

"Alexis, I want you to sit on the bench until you calm down," she said.

With only a few seconds left in the game, Stephanie scored the winning goal for the Bears.

"Oh, no!" thought Alexis. "By not playing fairly, I lost the big game for my team."

"We won, we won!" shouted the Bears. They lifted Stephanie high in the air.

"I'm sorry I didn't listen to you, Coach Barbie," said Alexis sadly. "Just because some people are unsportsmanlike doesn't mean I should be, too."

"It's all right," Barbie said. "If our team learned that lesson today, then we're all winners!"

The next day Barbie took her team to the beach. She
was surprised to see Skovoola setting up a photo shoot.
"Congratulations, Coach Barbie," said Skovoola. "So,
your Tigers won the big game!"

"Actually, we lost the game!" Barbie replied. "But we're celebrating because my Tigers learned a hard lesson: to be a *real* winner, you must play fairly. After all—it's not whether you win or lose, but how you play the game!"